This book is due for return on or before the last date shown below.

-5. JAN 1998	20. NOV. 2000
11. NOV. 1997	11. JAN 2002
-9. JAN 1998	
16. FEB. 1998	18. FEB. 2002
-9 NOV 1998	9/10/03
23. NOV 1998	
23. APR 1999	-7 OCT 2004
-. NOV. 1999	
15/11	14 FEB 2005
10. NOV. 2000	

Don Gresswell Ltd., London, N.21   Cat. No. 1208

To Charles, with love
Marie-Aline

© 1996 Editions Mango, Paris
First published in France by Mango, Paris in 1996
Tom va à l'école

© in this edition Evans Brothers Ltd 1997
Translation by Su Swallow
Reprinted 1997

First published in Great Britain by
Evans Brothers Ltd
2A Portman Mansions
Chiltern Street
London W1M 1LE

Printed in Belgium

0 237 51724 8

British Library Cataloguing in Publication Data.
A catalogue record for this book is available
from the British Library.

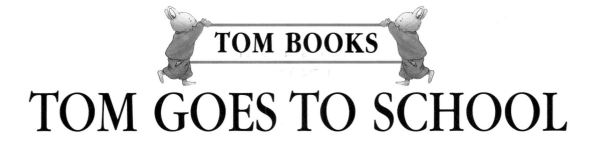

TOM BOOKS

TOM GOES TO SCHOOL

Illustrations by Marie-Aline Bawin
Written by Christophe Le Masne

Evans

Evans Brothers Limited

Tomorrow is my first day at school.
What will it be like? What will I do there?
I'm feeling very nervous.

Mummy and Daddy say
my teacher is very nice.
But how can they be so sure?
They don't really know her at all.

Mummy has bought me a pencil,
a rubber and some felt-tip pens.

And I've got a very smart satchel, too.
I love the smell of it, all new!

Mummy helps me to get all my things ready.
"Mummy, I think I feel ill.
I can't go to school tomorrow..."

So Mummy takes my temperature
and says I'm not ill at all.
But I really don't want to go tomorrow.

Time to say goodnight to Daddy.
"You are lucky to be going to school," he says.
"You will learn lots of exciting things."

When I go to bed, I ask Mummy if the teacher could come here, instead. My bedroom could be the classroom. The other children could come too. Mummy smiles and gives me a big hug.

I can't get to sleep.
I look at the moon through the window
and think about tomorrow...

"Wake up, sleepy head," says Mummy gently.
Oh dear, is it morning already?
I feel as though I have only just gone to sleep.

I've got butterflies in my stomach,
but I'm trying to be brave,
and I'm not going to cry!

On the way to school we meet lots of children.
I bet they are all trying not to cry, like me!

When we get to the school,
it's very hard to let go of Mummy.

"Take this," says Mummy, giving me
her handkerchief.
"Whenever you feel sad, just look at
it and think of me."

Here comes the teacher.
She looks very kind.
She takes us into school.
I hold on tight to Mummy's handkerchief.

This is our classroom.
It smells very clean and it looks very tidy.
What a lot of toys and books!

The boy next to me is called Alex.
He doesn't look very happy -
and now he is crying.

I try to cheer him up,
and I give him Mummy's
handkerchief to dry his tears.

In the morning, we do painting and
cutting out, and we sing songs.

At playtime, I play with Alex.
He's stopped crying,
and we have fun playing together.

In the afternoon, the teacher
tells us a story with puppets.
It's very funny!

Then the bell goes.
Is school finished already?

Mummy waits for me outside the school.
I'm really pleased to see her,
but I'm looking forward to tomorrow, too.
I want to play with Alex again, and finish my painting.